This Makes Me Happy

DEALING WITH FEELINGS

by Courtney Carbone
illustrated by Hilli Kushnir

Random House 🏠 New York

Today my class is going on
a field trip to the county fair!

We are all so excited!
It is hard to stay in our seats.

My teacher shows us
one way to relax.

4

We breathe in slowly.
We breathe out slowly.
Now I feel calm.

We get to the fair.
There is so much
to see and do!

6

I am so excited.
It feels like there are
butterflies in my tummy!

There is a long line
for the roller coaster.
We have to wait.
The line moves slowly.

But the ride is
worth the wait.
We go so fast.
I feel like I am flying!

Next, I get my face painted.
I ask the artist to paint
a yellow sun on my cheek.

She gives the sun
a big smile to match
the one on my face.

There is a pie-eating contest.
My teacher enters.

Three! Two! One!
The whistle blows.
We cheer her on.

She wins!
We jump up and down.

We see a glass jar
full of jelly beans.
It is a guessing game!

14

The jelly beans are every
color of the rainbow.
It feels like there is a rainbow
inside of me, too!

15

Then we go
to the petting zoo.

We help the farmer
feed the animals.
They tickle our hands.
I can't stop laughing!

We get to see a chick
hatch from her shell.

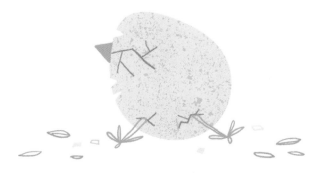

She is so small!
Cheep! Cheep!

The chick makes me feel
big and strong.
I can do anything!

There is a bake sale to support a good cause.

But I am allergic to nuts.
I cannot eat any
of the treats.

I feel left out.
My teacher sits down
next to me.
She has allergies, too.

She tells me not to worry.
We can still help out.
She is right!

It is time to go home.
We walk back to the bus
hand in hand.

What a great day!
My heart feels
like a hot-air balloon
high in the sky.

I have a good feeling
in my tummy.

But I did not have any treats!
What gave me this feeling?

Going on rides was exciting.

Playing games was a lot of fun.

Helping others made me feel good.

Many thoughts bounce around in my head.
I focus on them one at a time.

What am I feeling?
I am feeling HAPPY.

31

For kids everywhere, that they may find wonder and joy in being themselves

—*C.B.C.*

To Liam and Aya, whose genuine laughter always makes me HAPPY

—*H.K.*

Text copyright © 2018 by Courtney Carbone
Cover art and interior illustrations copyright © 2018 by Hilli Kushnir

All rights reserved. Published in the United States by Random House Children's Books, a division of Penguin Random House LLC, New York. Originally published by Rodale Kids, an imprint of Random House Children's Books, a division of Penguin Random House LLC, New York, in 2018.

Step into Reading, Random House, and the Random House colophon are registered trademarks of Penguin Random House LLC.

Visit us on the Web!
StepIntoReading.com
rhcbooks.com

Educators and librarians, for a variety of teaching tools, visit us at
RHTeachersLibrarians.com

Library of Congress Cataloging-in-Publication Data is available upon request.
ISBN 978-0-593-43420-8 (trade) — ISBN 978-0-593-43421-5 (lib. bdg.) —
ISBN 978-0-593-43422-2 (ebook)

Printed in the United States of America
10 9 8 7 6 5 4 3 2 1

This book has been officially leveled by using the F&P Text Level Gradient™ Leveling System.